THIS ITEM
BY PH
4/07

07.

26. 0

28.

18.

20

D1187241

C153091281

WITHDRAWN

Ben the Bully

Practising long vowel phonemes,
trisyllabic words and tricky words

First published in 2007 by
Franklin Watts
338 Euston Road
London
NW1 3BH

Franklin Watts Australia
Level 17/207 Kent Street
Sydney
NSW 2000

Text © Maggie Moore 2007
Illustration © Jan Smith 2007

The rights of Maggie Moore to be identified as the author
and Jan Smith as the illustrator of this Work have
been asserted in accordance with the Copyright, Designs
and Patents Act, 1988.

All rights reserved. No part of this publication may be
reproduced, stored in a retrieval system, or transmitted
in any form or by any means, electronic, mechanical,
photocopy, recording or otherwise, without the prior
written permission of the copyright owner.

A CIP catalogue record for this book is available
from the British Library.

ISBN: 978 0 7496 7284 3 (hbk)
ISBN: 978 0 7496 7322 2 (pbk)

Series Editor: Jackie Hamley
Series Advisors: Dr Barrie Wade, Dr Hilary Minns
Series Designer: Peter Scoulding

Printed in China

Franklin Watts is a division of
Hachette Children's Books.

KENT
LIBRARIES & ARCHIVES

C153091281

READING CORNER

PHONICS

Ben the Bully

by
Maggie Moore

Illustrated by
Jan Smith

W
FRANKLIN WATTS
LONDON•SYDNEY

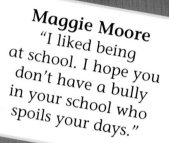

Maggie Moore
"I liked being at school. I hope you don't have a bully in your school who spoils your days."

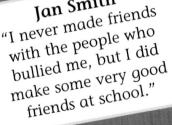

Jan Smith
"I never made friends with the people who bullied me, but I did make some very good friends at school."

When Jill rode her bike
outside, Ben, the bully, suddenly
gave her a push.

5

Jill began to cry, but Ben just gave a laugh and ran off.

At school, Jill said:

"Ben is a mean bully."

9

Ben drew with crayon
on Paul's painting.

He put Robin's lunch box
up on the bookshelf.

He made a splash in a puddle
with his wellingtons and made
Pat all wet.

Ben just gave a laugh
and ran off.

In the playground, nobody would play with Ben.

15

"Give me your football," Ben said.

"No!" said little Joe. "That is mean."

Ben suddenly felt sad.

He went away.

Nobody would sit near Ben.
"Goodness me!" said Miss Sweet
to Ben. "You must get help
with spelling!"

19

"I will help him," said little Joe.
So little Joe sat with Ben, helping
him with his spelling.

At lunchtime, Ben had
nobody to play with.

"I will play with him,"
said little Joe.

"Come and play with us!"
little Joe said to Paul and Jill.

So they played football.

"Come and play with us!"
Ben said to Robin and Pat.

27

"I'm sorry I was so mean," said Ben. "It was a joke."

"Well, it was not funny for us,"
they all said.

Now Ben is happy. He is not a bully and he is never mean.

Notes for parents and teachers

READING CORNER PHONICS has been structured to provide maximum support for children learning to read through synthetic phonics. The stories are designed for independent reading but may also be used by adults for sharing with young children.

The teaching of early reading through synthetic phonics focuses on the 44 sounds in the English language, and how these sounds correspond to their written form in the 26 letters of the alphabet. Carefully controlled vocabulary makes these books accessible for children at different stages of phonics teaching, progressing from simple CVC (consonant-vowel-consonant) words such as "top" (t-o-p) to trisyllabic words such as "messenger" (mess-en-ger). READING CORNER PHONICS allows children to read words in context, and also provides visual clues and repetition to further support their reading. These books will help develop the all important confidence in the new reader, and encourage a love of reading that will last a lifetime!

If you are reading this book with a child, here are a few tips:

1. Talk about the story before you start reading. Look at the cover and the title. What might the story be about? Why might the child like it?

2. Encourage the child to reread the story, and to retell the story in their own words, using the illustrations to remind them what has happened.

3. Discuss the story and see if the child can relate it to their own experience, or perhaps compare it to another story they know.

4. Give praise! Small mistakes need not always be corrected. If a child is stuck on a word, ask them to try and sound it out and then blend it together again, or model this yourself. For example "wish" w-i-sh "wish".

READING CORNER PHONICS covers two grades of synthetic phonics teaching, with three levels at each grade. Each level has a certain number of words per story, indicated by the number of bars on the spine of the book:

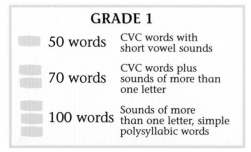

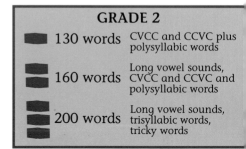